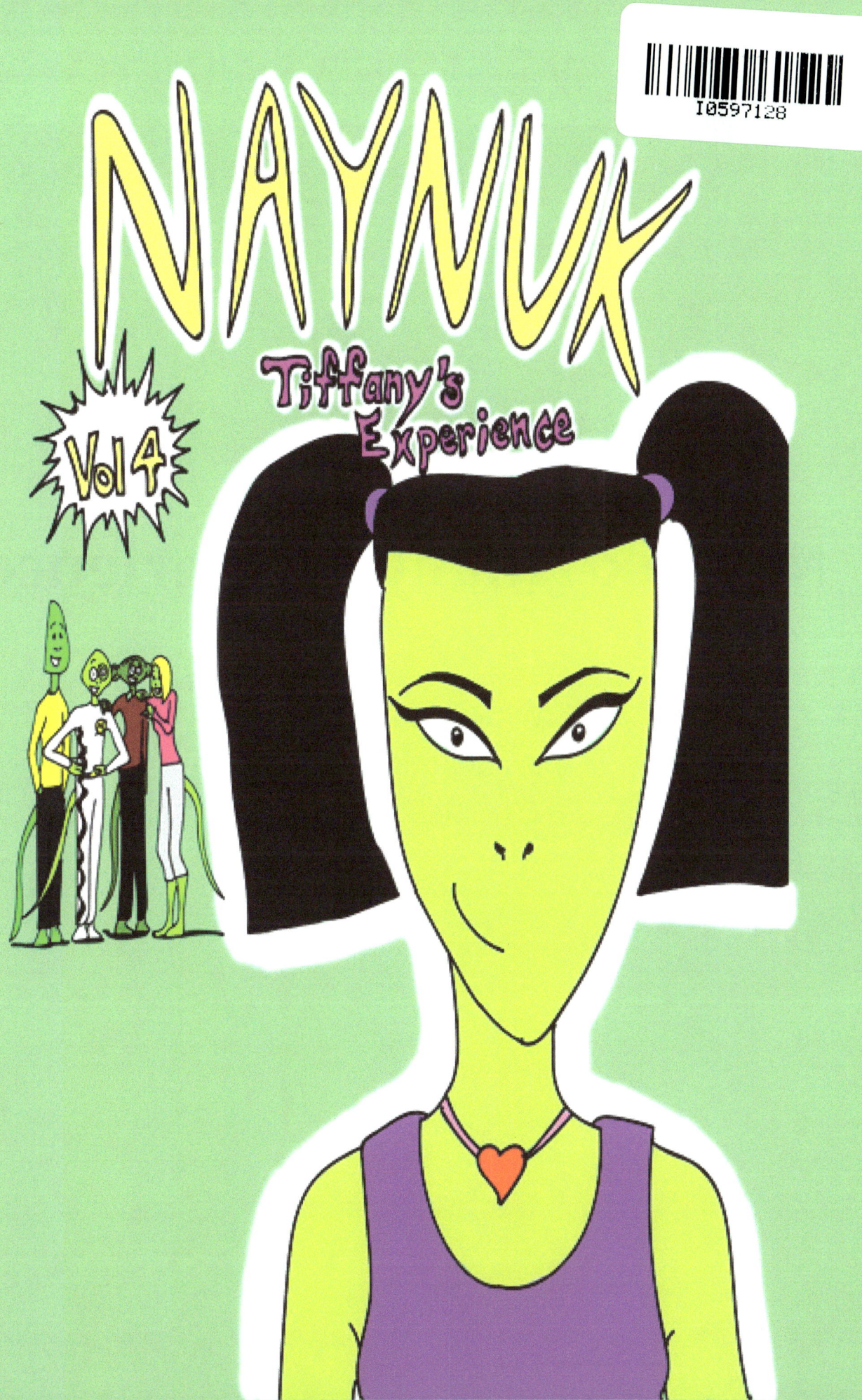

NAYNUK

Tiffany's Experience

Vol 4

Naynuk Tiffany's Experience©

Written and Illustrated by
Darrell Anthony McKinnon

Ravishing Gecko Publishing
Fourth Edition 2019
Copyright© by Darrell Anthony McKinnon
First Published by Darrell Anthony McKinnon
Duluth, Georgia, 30096 USA www.ravishinggecko.com

ISBN: 978-0-9989938-6-7 (Soft Cover)
ISBN: 978-0-9989938-7-4 (eBook)

McKinnon, Darrell A.
Naynuk Tiffany's Experience/ by Darrell Anthony McKinnon

Children's/Young Adults/Adults Christian Comic Book

Editor
Cait Patterson

This book is dedicated to
THE FATHER, THE SON, AND THE HOLY SPIRIT.
"I love them because they loved me first."

Out of nowhere a small voice intercepts, it's Tiffany.

He turns around in shock and says.

"When two are more stand in agreement on anything they shall ask, it shall be done in Jesus name. I'm with you Naynuk, we are ready!"

"TIFFANY!"

"You're not meant to do this by yourself. You encouraged me eariler."

The battle starts: Both pairs move, dodge, and fight with vigor, force, and power. The warriors turn the parking lot inside out.

Zonk, Zora, Toothy, and the other customers look outside in shock and awe.

Zonk looks at Toothy and Zora and say.

"We can't just sit on the sidelines and be scared. We have to get out of our comfort zones. If Tiffany believed we can too!"

"I agree, Christ Jesus taught us that we will endure a lot, but we must deny ourselves and stand firm! Remember, we are more than conquerors in Christ Jesus!"

"YEAH!!"

The other customers look at the three and cheer them on. But suddenly, a loud noise comes from outside. Zonk, Zora, Toothy, and the other customers stop and focus outside.

Naynuk and Tiffany in The Holy Spirit, together form a massive stream of light and throw it at Pitzel and Jinxx, catching them off guard knocking them across the parking lot.

The two foes get up.

"We must regroup, Pitzel. When we battle again we will have a full team. You've been warned; be aware!"

The two foes run off into nowhere

"Are you okay?"

"YEAH"

The customers come outside as well to cheer them on.
"YEAH!"
"YEAH!"
Squ

Meanwhile Jinxx and Pitzel make it back to their hideout.

"I wasn't expecting that. Who is she and where did she come from?"

"That's a good question, Jinxx. We've got to be prepared and come back even harder!"

"Don't worry, I have just the two who can help. I'll call up two of my buddies I know from a long. . . time ago: Boxer and Regret."

As Tiffany continues to blush profusely she says.

"Zonk's right, you defintely inspired me and made me believe in myself."

Tiffany gives Naynuk a massive hug and a kiss as Naynuk blushes in shyness.

"WOW! Where did that come from?!"

"I don't know."

Zonk looks at Zora and smiles as Zora smiles back. Then quickly her expression turns serious.

The crew laughs together.

Naynuk smiles and shakes his head, out of the corner of his eye he sees Zonk and Toothy peeking out of their cubicles, also smiling.

Naynuk still smiling, laughs and puts his head down, trying not to be noticed by other co-workers.

Mr. Terry comes over and cuts the funny moment.

"What's so funny?"

Naynuk cuts his laughter quickly.

"Oh, it's nothing, Mr. Terry. I'm just being silly."

"Make sure that work gets completed."

"Yes Sir!"

He sees the crew laughing and turn back toward their cubicles.

"Sounds good to me."

Tiffany and Zora are chatting, as Zora sees the three come in.

Zora puts her hand over her mouth and cuts her eye toward the fellows, grinning and whispering to Tiffany.

Zonk walks over toward the giggling two, followed by Naynuk and Toothy and says.

"What's so funny ladies."

"You three obviously."

Tiffany follows, as usual, putting her hand over her mouth with that cute sniffle she does.

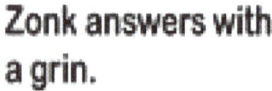

Zonk answers with a grin.

"You guys are so wierd."

"Long time no see, bro. As far as life, it's never been better!"

"Hey bro, would you be in the mood of doing your old buddy old pal a huge. . . favor, like old times?"

"Why sure, we're brothers for life."

"Well let's meet tomorrow. I may be having another partner join us. You may very well know him."

"That's cool with me, the more the merrier."

Jinxx hangs up the phone and makes a call to another old time friend Regret.

Regret answers the phone.

"May I ask with whom I'm speaking with?"

"Just take a wild guess."

Regret responds back numerous times and says.

"I don't know, but I tell you once you reveal yourself, you better hope I know who you are or you will regret ever calling me,"

"Oh I won't regret it. It's me, your old mate Jinxx!"

Regret is shocked. He laughs and says.

"Oh goodness, bro it's been a very long. . . time. Wow!"

"Yes. . . listen I may need a favor, old buddy. Are you up for that?!"

Then Jinxx goes on to explain the favor.

Meanwhile back at Crosspointe Times.

The work day is about to end and Mr. Terry is having a meeting with the team.

"Next week will be very busy, so I need every one to come ready and willing, pronto, okay? You guys are dismissed."

The crew comes together to plan for the weekend.

"Does anyone have any ideas for the weekend?"

"No worries, we'll figure something out when it gets closer."

Everyone agrees

"Okay guys, I'm about to go, it's been a long. . . day."

"Ooo. .I can just feel it now brewing in me! Let Jinxx and his posse come. I'm ready for them!"

"Slow down, slow down. There will be a time when it comes, and I will be ready too."

As the two stop in front of Tiffany's door, Tiffany says.

"I'm so glad I believed you and God's word. I can never lose faith in the truth, with what I've witnessed."

"Well that is our mission, spreading the word and making more witnesses."

"Well, I'm going inside. I'll see you tomorrow."

As she gives Naynuk a special kiss on the cheek and a hug.

The bully turns and says.
“Get out of here. It’s none of your business.
The small guy says.
“Help me please! Help me!”
“Let him go please!”
“I’m telling you butt out, or else!”

Naynuk walks over to the small guy and helps him up and says.

"Are you okay, mister?"

"Yes thank you. If you hadn't come, I don't know what I would've done."

"I was here for a reason."

Naynuk helps the small guy up and sees him inside his home safely.

Naynuk goes over to Mrs. Beverly's to visit and have some company.

Out of curiousity he asks Mrs. Beverly.

"Mrs. Beverly, If you acquired super powers, what would you do with them? How would you feel? How would you use them?

"Well, I know I would go crazy over the things I could do. Nevermind, let me stop be funny. There is one big thing If i had powers. I would want to do good for others, and would like to be a good role model."

He thinks and wonders to himself.

"That's a good answer! Well, I've got to get up early, but thanks, Mrs. Beverly!"

He dashes to his apartment next door.

As he gets to his room, he gets on his tablet and googles inspirational scriptures on doing good.

Meanwhile, Tiffany calls Zora amd continues ranting on about how awesome she felt when The Holy Spirit was over her.

"I can imagine. I would love to feel that."

"Yes I do, Tiffany, I do."

"It's like fire! I felt like another person. I felt extra strong! It's unbeliveable, Zora!"

"You can! All you have to do is believe!"

They smile together. Meanwhile back at Jinxx's hideout Pitzel, Boxer, and Regret are planning their next showdown.

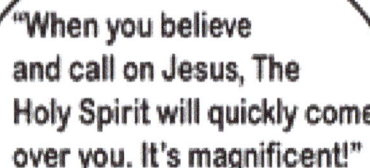

"When you believe and call on Jesus, The Holy Spirit will quickly come over you. It's magnificent!"

Pitzel introduces himself to Boxer and Regret as they share the respect back.

"Okay, okay let's get on with it. I think Pitzel and me need to distract the two, and they won't expect another pair to come to our defense. Those two are extremely powerful together, so I made you guys the same plasma bracelets we have."

"These bracelets are very powerful and strong. I heard you guys love power."

"That is very true. It gives me a sense of authority."

"Yes. . .likewise. There's a reason I was given this name: I won't them to regret they ever messed with me."

"That's the spirit! With this team, they won't stand a chance!"

"Oh. . .yeah we're ready. Let's do this!"

They run out of the house excited and hyped up.

Back at Squeaky Beats the crew sits together and relaxes.

"I'm glad Mr. Terry was pleased with our work."

"I know right."

"What are you guys thinking about ordering?"

The crew is shocked, but Naynuk instantly gets strong in the spirit and says.

"Also, I told you I would be ready!"

Tiffany follows and says.

"That's right, and he's not alone! I'm strong in the spirit now!"

"You two are very powerful together, but now I have extra help. We've even the odds!"

Naynuk and Tiffany stand up from the table and say.

"BRING IT!"

Pitzel shoots a plasma ball at Tiffany, knocking her back on the table.

Naynuk's suit quickly appears on him as he grows in muscle mass and says.

"No way, you've done it now!"

Tiffany gets up angryily, pulsing in the spirit as Naynuk quickly flies into Pitzel carrying him through the door outside. Tiffany follows quickly, flying into Jinxx, carrying him outside as well.

Boxer and Regret quickly run outside behind the two.

Outside of Squeaky Beats, the two pairs fight it out.

Boxer and Regret join in, plasma balls and streams of light coming from everywhere.

The customers look outside the window in suspense.

Zonk turns to Toothy and Zora and says.

"Remember what happened last time and what we could've done?! It's our time to believe and call on The Holy Spirit to empower us!"

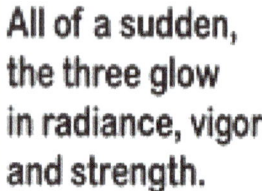

"Yes! Yes! It's unreal!"

"Let's go and save our friends!"

The three put their hands together and say.

The crew runs outside quickly as the customers look on.

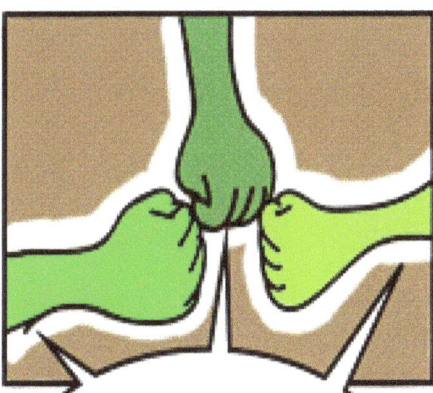

"Go team Spirit go!"

To be continued. . . .

www.ingramcontent.com/pod-product-compliance
Lightning Source LLC
Chambersburg PA
CBHW042013120726
47911CB00029B/915